Hippo and Duck Bedtime Stories

Hippo and Duck
Bedtime Stories

Michael Cole

Introduction by Chris Serle
Illustrations by John Haslam

THE ULTIMATE SLEEP SYSTEM

MICHAEL O'MARA BOOKS LIMITED

First published in Great Britain by
Michael O'Mara Books Limited
20 Queen Anne Street
London W1N 9FB

British Library Cataloguing Publication Data

Cole, Michael, *1933 –*
    Hippo and Duck Bedtime Stories
    I. Title
    823′.914[J]

    ISBN 0–948397–88–8

Filmset by DP Photosetting, Aylesbury, Bucks.
Printed and bound by Arti Grafiche Motta s.p.a, Milan

INTRODUCTION BY CHRIS SERLE

By buying this book you are helping World Wide Fund For Nature (WWF) to save animals in Africa. The money we raise will be helping a project in Zambia, where the lives of hippos and other animals are being threatened by poaching and agricultural development on their environment. WWF are developing a plan to protect the rich natural resources of the area so that animals and humans can live successfully alongside each other.

With your support we are on the way to raising the money we need.

To thank you for your support Silentnight are offering you the chance to see the hippo project in action with a 2 week holiday prize to Zambia. All you have to do is enter the colouring competition in the back of the book.

Good luck and thank you.

Best wishes Chris Serle x

The Skiers

Hippo and Duck had gone up into the hills for a skiing holiday. But when they got there, there was no snow. They felt sad.

'We can't ski without snow,' said Hippo.

'We can't throw snowballs, or even make a snowman without snow,' said Duck.

'What *can* we do without snow?'

'Nothing,' said Hippo. 'Except dream about it.'

So they went to bed feeling very fed up. They dreamt about snow.

In the morning they found that their dream had come true. During the night, heavy snow had fallen, and the hills were covered with a thick carpet. 'Just right for skiing,' said Hippo.

They had a quick breakfast and went out onto the slopes.

Soon, the new snow, which didn't even have a footprint on it, was criss-crossed with the tracks of their skis. They made patterns with them.

Duck's tracks were close together, and Hippo's wide apart. Then they climbed higher to where the slopes were steeper.

Hippo stood at the top of the steepest slope and looked down into the valley below. 'I'm going to jump this one,' he said. 'If I go fast enough, I'll be able to take off. I'll fly through the air, and land down there.'

'Are you sure it's safe?' asked Duck.

'It's safe for me,' replied Hippo. 'But not for you. I've done it many times before. In fact I was ski-jump champion in 19 ... er ... I've forgotten the exact date. It's not too difficult to learn. You stand here and watch.'

Hippo came rushing downhill. He took off into the air just at the spot where Duck was standing. Duck was very worried about her friend, and flew off after him to make sure he was all right.

She needn't have worried. Hippo knew exactly what he was doing, and made a perfect landing. And then Duck made a perfect landing too – on Hippo's shoulder!

'I told you not to jump!' said Hippo.

'I didn't jump,' said Duck. 'I flew. You seem to forget sometimes that I have wings!'

They both laughed. And before they went indoors, they made a large snowman – or rather, a large Snowhippo – with a Snowduck on his shoulder!

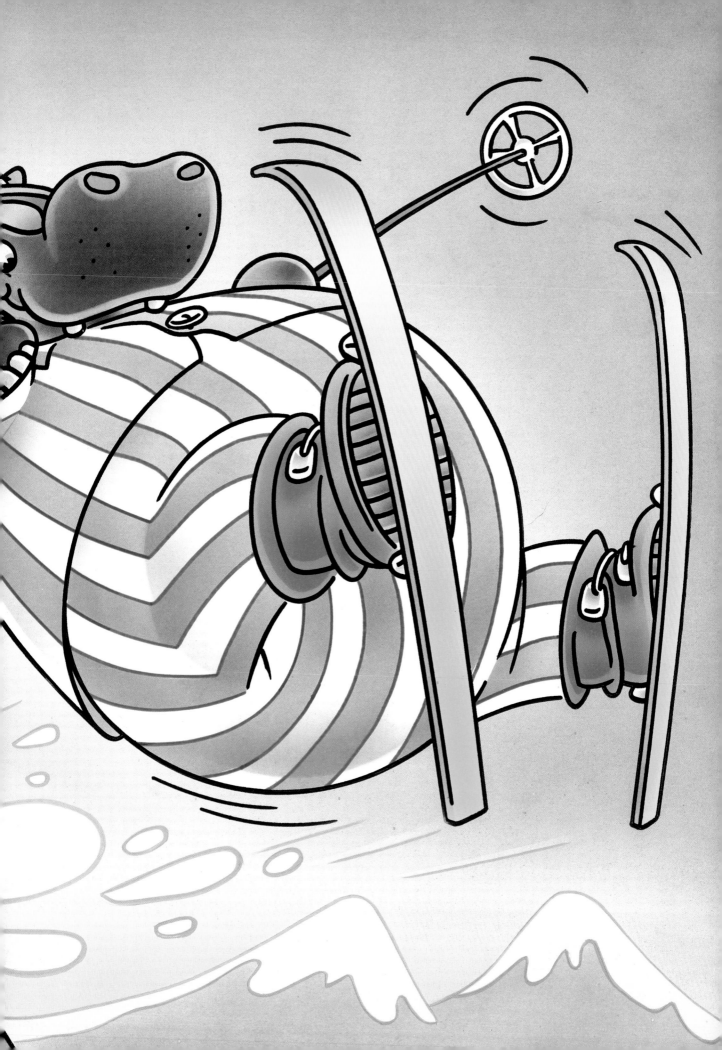

The Fair

When Duck came home one day, she was hopping up and down with excitement, and shouting at the top of her voice: 'The Fair has come to town! The Fair has come to town!'

Hippo, who had been having a quiet snooze in his chair, woke with a start and said, 'There's no need to shout!'

'The fair has come to town,' whispered Duck.

'And there's no need to make a secret of it, either,' said Hippo.

He stood up. 'Well, if the Fair's come to town, we should go to town too,' he said.

They took a bus to the fair, getting more and more excited the nearer they came.

As soon as they entered the fairground, they bought some candyfloss. Duck's was so big she looked like a ball of candyfloss with legs on.

Then they went on the Merry-go-round, which was made up of different animals. Duck sat on a hippo, and Hippo sat on a big duck. It went round so fast that Hippo soon got giddy. But the faster it went, the more Duck liked it. Hippo walked off feeling so dizzy that he started banging into things. Duck had another go.

Then they went on the Bumper cars. Hippo liked that better. He bumped Duck eight times, and Duck bumped him six. Hippo wanted another go, but Duck wanted to go on the Big Dipper. So Hippo stayed in his bumper car while Duck had as many thrills as she could take on the Big Dipper.

Next they went to the coconut shy. Duck won so many coconuts she couldn't carry them. Hippo threw the balls much harder, but missed every time. 'Never mind,' said Duck. 'You can share mine. We'll have coconut sandwiches and coconut milk for tea!' But the last thing they tried was the best fun of all. They went into the Hall of Mirrors, which, if you were fat, made you look thin, and if you were thin, made you look fat. If you were big they made you look small, and if you were small, the magic mirrors made you look big. They made Duck look bigger than Hippo!

They laughed and laughed at the funny sight, and couldn't stop laughing all the way home on the bus. They even laughed through their coconut tea!

The Shade

It was a beautiful day, and Hippo and Duck were up early. They had planned to go for a long walk in the country and take a picnic.

Hippo made some very large sandwiches for himself, and some very small sandwiches for Duck. He put them in his knapsack, picked up his walking stick, and they set off.

The sun was still low in the sky as they crossed the fields. It made their shadows, and the shadows of the trees, very long.

'Look how big my shadow is!' said Duck.

'And look how big mine is,' said Hippo.

As they walked, the sun rose higher in the sky, and their shadows grew shorter.

'Look how short my shadow is now!' said Duck.

'And look how short mine is!' said Hippo.

The sun felt much hotter now, and Duck and Hippo began to feel tired.

'What time is it?' Duck asked Hippo.

'Lunch time,' said Hippo. 'Let's sit down in the sun and have our picnic.' And he sat down.

'No, let's sit in the shade,' said Duck, who was feeling far too hot.

'Let's go over there and sit in the shade of that tree.'

'You go and sit in the shade if you like,' said Hippo, who didn't feel like moving. He had found a nice, soft patch of grass to sit on. 'Do you mind if I carry on sitting here? I like to feel the sun on me.'

'It's a shame not to have our picnic together,' said Duck. 'Especially after coming all this way.' She sounded very sad.

They sat and thought. Then Hippo had an idea.

'I know,' he said. 'I'll sit in the sun, and you can sit in the shadow I'm making. That way we can have the best of both worlds.'

So they sat there and ate their sandwiches – Hippo enjoying the sun, and Duck enjoying the shade.

After lunch, the sun grew even hotter.

'Now even I am finding the sun too hot,' said Hippo.

'Well, you can't sit in my shade, I'm afraid,' said Duck. 'My shadow's not big enough. Why don't you go and sit in the shade of that tree?'

'I'm going to do better than that,' said Hippo. 'I'm going for a swim in the river.'

'I'll join you in a minute,' said Duck. 'I like to get *really* hot before I go in the water.'

The Party

Duck and Hippo had been so busy decorating their house that they had seen very little of their friends. 'Let's have a party,' said Duck, 'and invite them all.' 'Good idea,' said Hippo. 'But we must have a name for the party. I mean it's not a birthday party, or anything like that, but it must be a *something* party.' 'Let's call it a "Hello" Party,' said Duck. 'Good idea,' said Hippo. 'We must make invitations.'
So they got busy with paper and colours, and made lots of bright invitations. Then Duck flew off with them and dropped them down to their friends.

'Now we must decorate the house,' said Duck, when she came back.

'We've just done that,' said Hippo.

'No, I mean for the party,' said Duck. 'We'll need some balloons.'

'Good idea,' said Hippo, and he went out to buy balloons.

They had a job blowing them up. Hippo blew so hard that most of his balloons burst. Duck used all her breath to blow up one balloon, then she felt tired. But in the end they blew them all up.

'Now for the food,' said Duck. 'I think we should have jelly.'

'Yes!' said Hippo. 'Let's make a little jelly to look just like you, and a big one to look just like me. And they made a duck jelly, and a hippo jelly.

'Now what games shall we play at the party?' asked Duck.

'We must make a picture of a donkey, and then make a tail. Everybody should try to pin the tail on to the right end of the donkey. They have to wear a blindfold, too.'

'If you don't mind my saying so,' said Duck, 'I think it would be funnier if we made a picture of a Hippo and got everyone to pin a tail on that.' Hippo agreed, and chuckled all the time they were making the picture. Then suddenly, he stopped laughing. He looked very serious.

'What's the matter?'
asked Duck.
'Well,' said Hippo.
'I've just had
a thought. My friends
all tend to be rather … er …
large – so much larger than your
friends that in a crowded room your
friends might get … well … squashed.'
'No problem,' said Duck.
'We'll use the big table.
I and my friends will have our party
under the table, where we'll be safe.
We'll have our duck jelly there. And you
and your friends can have your party round
the table with the hippo jelly on it.
And we'll take it in turns to play games.'
'Good idea,' said Hippo.
And that's what they did. Everyone thought
it was the best 'Hello' Party they had ever
been to!

The Kite

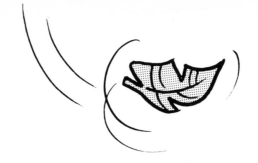

It was a very windy day. 'It's too windy to go for a walk,' said Hippo. 'It's too windy to go for a swim,' said Duck. 'I prefer to stay in and watch the clouds blow by through the window.'
'But we should get out for a bit,' said Hippo. 'It will blow the cobwebs away.' 'It will blow us away too,' said Duck. Then suddenly, she remembered the kites they had flown last summer. They were in the attic. She brought them down. They were still as good as new.
Duck's kite had a duck bigger than herself painted on it.
Hippo's kite had a hippo smaller than himself painted on it.
They went out with their kites, walking against the wind. It was so strong, it blew Duck backwards. 'Walk behind me,' said Hippo. 'That way you'll be out of the worst of the wind.' And so, with Hippo leading and Duck following, they reached the top of the hill.

'I'll send my kite up first,' said Hippo. 'We'll see what the wind does to it. I don't want yours to get damaged.'

The kite went up without any problem, and the wind made it dance in the air. Higher and higher it went. 'Now let yours go,' said Hippo. 'But hold tight!'

Up went Duck's kite dancing as merrily as Hippo's. But suddenly, an extra strong gust of wind blew up and took the kite with such force that it snatched the string out of Duck's hands.

'Oh dear, oh dear!' said Duck. She started running after it. Hippo drew his kite in, and followed Duck. The kite darted madly about in the wind, then landed at the top of a tall tree.

'Don't worry,' said Hippo. 'I'll get it back for you.' And he started to climb the tree. He was all right climbing the thick branches, but when he got higher, the branches were thinner. Hippo's weight was too great for him to climb any further.

'Don't climb any higher!' said Duck, worried that her friend might fall. 'I'll fly up and knock the kite down to you.'

Duck flew up to the top of the tree and tapped the kite with her beak until it was freed from the twigs. It fell into the waiting arms of Hippo down below. Then Hippo climbed carefully down to the ground with the kite, and they went home to tea. That evening, they couldn't stop talking about what a wonderful afternoon they had had in the wind!

The Swim

It was another hot day. 'Let's go to the seaside for a swim,' said Hippo.
'The seaside's too far,' said Duck. 'I just can't wait to get into the water.'
'All right then,' agreed Hippo. 'Let's go to the river.'
But everybody else had thought of going to the river too. It was crowded with swimmers, and boats of every shape and size. Hippo and Duck walked and walked until they found a quieter spot. They changed into their costumes, and Hippo put a toe in the water.
'It's too cold to go in,' he said.
'Don't be silly,' said Duck. 'It's just right.'
She went into the water, and splashed Hippo, who was still standing on the edge. Hippo had to laugh. Then he jumped into the water with a great splash, and started to chase Duck.

Hippo was so large that when he swam he made great waves in the river. The waves annoyed someone who was fishing on the opposite bank. 'Easy there,' he said. 'You'll frighten all the fish. Go and swim somewhere else!'

They went further down the river, but Hippo's waves rocked the boats.

'Easy there!' the people said, as their boats went up and down. 'You'll tip us out. Go and swim somewhere else!'

'But there is nowhere else,' said Duck.

'Yes there is,' said Hippo. 'The seaside. Come on!'

The two friends climbed onto the bank and changed. Then they went to the station and caught the next train to the seaside.

But by the time they arrived, a stiff breeze had sprung up. The sea was full of white waves.
'Look at those waves!' said Duck. 'It's far too rough to swim.'
'Nonsense,' said Hippo. 'It's quite safe. Look at everyone else in the water. Besides, the waves make it more fun. Come on! You can start on my back.'
So Hippo started to swim with Duck on his back. Duck could see that the waves weren't so big once you were in them. She jumped off to swim on her own. 'This beats the river . . . oops!' she said, going up and down on a big wave, '. . . any day!'

WIN A TRIP TO SEE HIPPOS IN THE WILD

WIN A TRIP TO SEE HIPPOS IN THE WILD

Silentnight together with WWF, Abercrombie & Kent and Zambian Airways are offering a fabulous two week holiday for two to see the hippos in Zambia. Money raised by this book will be helping save hippos and other animals in the Kafue Flats in Zambia. The holiday trip will include a safari to a special project at Kafue Flats plus there will be a visit to the Luangwa Valley where you will see many animals including hippo, leopard, elephant, lion, giraffe, zebra and many species of birds.

All you have to do is colour in the hippo and duck picture opposite and complete the tie breaker then very carefully cut out the page from your book and send it to Silentnight Ltd, WWF/B Competition, PO Box 9, Barnoldswick, Colne, Lancashire BB8 6BL.

6 runners up will receive a cuddly hippo. Vital statistics: Chest: 22in. Height: 21in. Retail value £39.95.

Entry to the competition means you become a 'Friend of the Hippo' and you will receive a letter and badge to thank you for your support.

Competition Rules

1) The judge's decision will be final and no correspondence will be entered into.
2) Age will be taken into consideration.
3) A winner under the age of 16 will be required to be accompanied by an adult on the holiday.
4) Employees (and their immediate relatives) of Silentnight Ltd, Abercrombie & Kent and Zambian Airways, and their associated companies are not eligible to enter.
5) Closing date 31st March 1989.
6) Winners will be notified by post.
7) Complete the tie breaker

Don't forget to fill in the tie breaker and your name and address on the back of your coloured picture.